Babar characters TM & © 1990 L. de Brunhoff
All rights reserved
Based on the animated series "Babar"
A Nelvana-Ellipse Presentation
a Nelvana Production in Association with The Clifford Ross Company, Ltd

# Based on characters created
# by Jean and Laurent de Brunhoff

Based on a story by Templeton and Crawford
Image adaptation by Van Gool-Lefèvre-Loiseaux
Produced by Twin Books U.K. Ltd, London

This 1990 edition published by JellyBean Press,
distributed by Outlet Book Company, Inc.,
a Random House Company,
225 Park Avenue South
New York NY 10003

ISBN 0-517-052067

8 7 6 5 4 3 2 1

Printed and bound in Barcelona, Spain by Cronion, S.A.

# BABAR

# The Show Must Go On

JellyBean Press
New York

A great theatrical event was in the making at Babar's palace. All the children were involved. Pom and Alexander were actors, and Flora was the director.

The only ones in the audience, for the moment, were their parents.

The children rehearsed one scene over and over again, and their tempers were getting short.

Alexander thought his part had too many words, so he kept leaving them out, but Flora wouldn't cut a single line.

"Okay! If you won't do that for me," said the naughty little elephant, "I quit."

Flora was very discouraged. "If they won't follow my direction," she said unhappily to her father, "what can I do?"

Babar said, "In the theater, the director is in charge. Everyone else must follow his instructions. There is no room for arrogance or laziness."

"I must say," Babar added, "that Alexander's behavior reminds me of a time when I was young...

"...We had managed, after many efforts, to arrange a performance right here in Celesteville, by the famous ballerina Rosa Anastasia Soretoza. It was a great honor."

10

But such a production also included a lot of worries. When Babar introduced his friends to the star at a party in her honor, he found out that she was proud as a peacock!

As one might imagine, the dancer was very popular, and even before rehearsals began, every ticket was sold. Success was assured.

Assured, but for one thing. This queen of dancers was not an easy person to please. The first time something was not to her liking, she stalked off to her dressing room and buried her head in a pile of sand. She sulked this way all night long.

Finally, Babar came to her dressing room and asked, "What seems to be the problem, Madame?"

"It's not my problem, it's HIS," Madame Soretoza shrieked, pointing to the director. "He wants me to wear this dreadful costume."

"It's the costume which is always worn in this ballet," replied the director. "Every other ballerina has worn one just like it. But there is no reason to go over the subject again. It's very simple. If you don't wear it, I quit."

"Good riddance!" replied the furious dancer.

And the director left.

"Who will replace him?" asked Babar, who was getting worried.

"Who else but you, yourself, Your Majesty," said the dancer. "Don't worry. I'll tell you what to do, and you just follow my orders. It's really very simple."

Meanwhile, in the palace of Rataxes, king of the rhinoceroses, Lady Rataxes was getting angry.

"I'm married to a barbarian," she wailed. "A man who would rather duel with one of his courtiers than take me to see Soretoza dance. I am nothing to him! I'm so miserable."

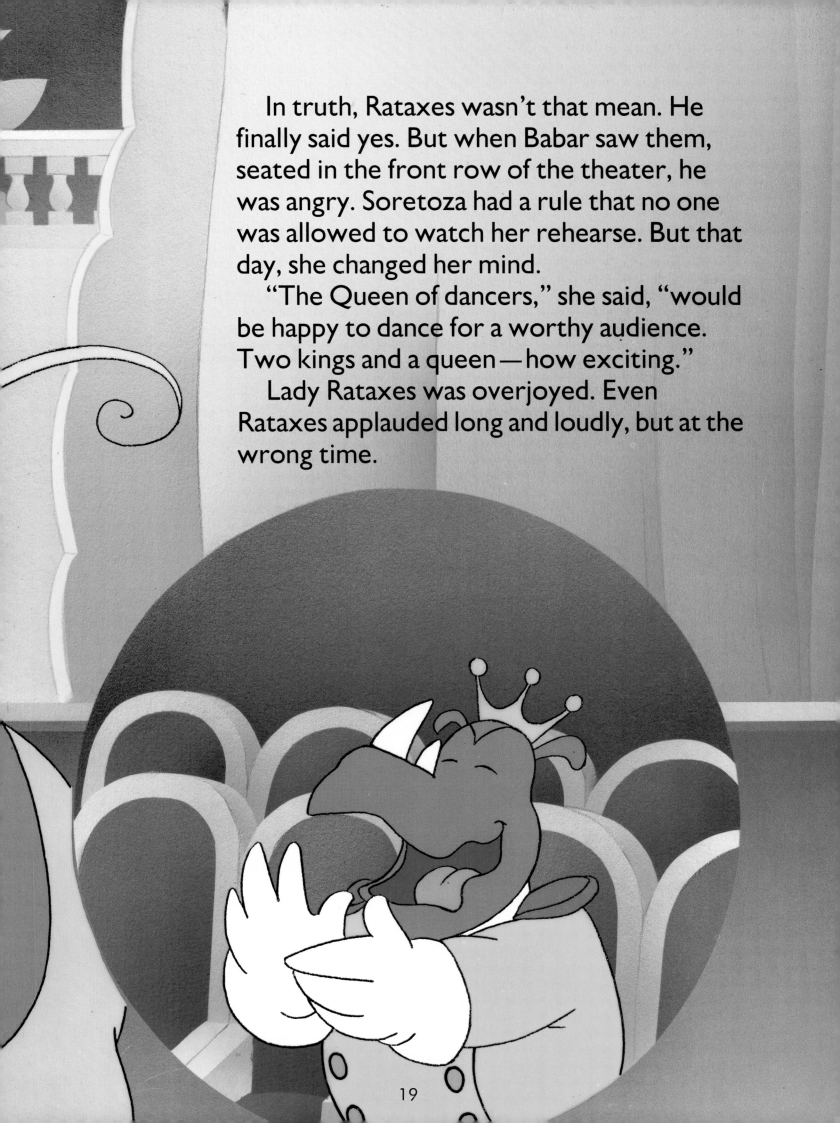

In truth, Rataxes wasn't that mean. He finally said yes. But when Babar saw them, seated in the front row of the theater, he was angry. Soretoza had a rule that no one was allowed to watch her rehearse. But that day, she changed her mind.

"The Queen of dancers," she said, "would be happy to dance for a worthy audience. Two kings and a queen—how exciting."

Lady Rataxes was overjoyed. Even Rataxes applauded long and loudly, but at the wrong time.

20

Unfortunately, the happy moment did not last. This time the lighting did not please Madame Soretoza.

"What can that electrician be thinking of?" she shrieked. "A blue spotlight! Nothing could be less becoming to one with my delicate coloring. Dismiss him immediately. If he doesn't go, I will!"

Babar tried to defend the electrician, but it was useless. The minute Babar opened his mouth, the "Great Artiste" returned to her dressing room, to sulk with her head in the box of sand.

The date of the great production grew nearer and nearer.
To lose even a single day of rehearsal might spell disaster.
Celeste had an idea.

"I could replace Madame Soretoza for the rehearsals," she
suggested shyly. "Then you will be able to continue directing
the rest of the ballet."

Everything would have been fine if Soretoza had stayed away. But the minute she heard the music, she returned—only to make fun of her understudy. Poor Celeste! She was so embarrassed, she burst into tears.

Babar gave her a hug and told her she was dancing beautifully. He told everyone else to ignore Madame Soretoza. They would continue with the rehearsals whether she liked it or not.

The new plan worked well, for a while. Madame Soretoza rehearsed properly, until the day she slipped on the staircase. She instantly blamed her fall on Leon, the conductor, saying he had miscued the orchestra. Leon did not bother to reply. He simply broke his baton and walked out the door.

Thus, by the last day of rehearsals, the brilliant company was reduced to nothing. But Babar found that his friends were ready to work miracles. They all knew the show must go on. Babar called them together and gave each one a job to do in the theater. Arthur took over sound, and Cornelius became the conductor. Zephir opened and closed the curtain. Pompadour went to the switchboard to run the lights. Celeste took over make-up, and the Old Lady was in charge of costumes.

25

"Thank you, my friends!" said Babar after the last rehearsal. "Now I think everything will be perfect, thanks to your hard work and good will. On stage and behind the scenes, from young and old alike, I've never seen such an array of talent. And among all of us, not even a hint of a tantrum."

Babar continued his speech: "Nothing can stop us now. Not even lack of cooperation from our star. We didn't take that seriously, right, Celeste?

29

"To understudy the prima ballerina, and make up the entire company as well, takes a lot of skill and patience.

"To design lighting that looks like daylight takes talent that I didn't know you had, Pompadour. One false step and a short circuit could cut out all our lights. We don't have just one star. We have a company of stars. I'm proud of you all."

Everything seemed to be going well. Nevertheless, there was one problem. The great star was still sulking, and saying rude and discouraging things to the stage crew.

"Your company," she finally said to Babar, "is not professional. A dancer with great talent like mine does not work with amateurs. I'm telling you this for your own good. Get me a real company to work with. Otherwise, I don't dance."

"Very well," said Babar. "I'm sorry you feel that way. But *your* behavior hasn't been very professional. In fact, you've been acting like a spoiled brat. If you wish to leave, the door is wide open."

The great star turned bright red. Furiously, she spun around on her heels and left. And this time she didn't return.

"Celeste, you will replace her," said Pompadour. "You dance as well as she does! But what about a partner?" he added with horror. "That role was never cast. Who will take it? What will we do?"

"Now I will let you in on a little secret," said Babar proudly.

35

Several seconds later, the company discovered the fabulous
surprise that Babar had arranged. The dancer in question
was—Rataxes! Babar had been rehearsing him in secret, and
he made a great impression in his beautiful costume and
plumed hat.

Opening night arrived, and all Celesteville came to the theater to see the ballet with a new star — the rhinoceros king. His wife was delighted.

Seated in one of the boxes,
with Basil, Lady Rataxes was
thrilled by the performance.

The entire ballet was a great success, from the first thrill of the violins during the overture to the brilliantly danced finale, when Celeste leaped into the arms of the lead dancer.

39

The great Soretoza was forgotten. The audience stood on the seats and applauded the performers for 15 minutes, throwing enormous bouquets onto the stage. After all the worry, Babar and his company had earned their ovation. But never in their wildest dreams had they imagined they would have such a success.

"And it happened because we all worked together, and no one sulked or misbehaved," concluded Babar.

"It's a pity when someone is arrogant and too proud like Soretoza and doesn't understand that the show must go on. Because pleasing the audience is what the theater is all about."

"Oh, Alexander, please try," sighed Flora sadly.

"I think I understand now," said her little brother. "I'll try as hard as I can, even if I do find the part too long."

"Bravo!" cried Flora, once again the director.

"I think it might be a little early for congratulations," said Babar gently.

But several days later, when the play opened, Alexander knew every single one of his lines from beginning to end, without prompting. His father and mother were very proud of him, and of all the children. Remembering the good old days, they applauded long and loudly.